Eleanor Taylor

Beep, Beep, Let's Go!

BLOOMSBURY
CHILDREN'S
BOOKS

'Jump in. Buckle up. All set?

Let's go!'

Beep Beep

'Bye bye!'

Squeak
Squeak

'You too?'

Beep Beep Chugga Chugga Beep Beep

Zebras crossing.

'Wait awhile.'

Beep Beep Chugga Chugga Chugga

Honk Honk Moo Moo

'Up the hill, slowly now . . .

Down the hill, fast as you can!'

'I spy . . .

...the seaside!'

Towels, hats

and beachtime snacks.

'Run fast.'
Sandy toes.

'Jump in!'

Big splash!